Eleanor Mason's Literary Adventures
writing journal
copyright 2022
Poison Apple Press, LLC

POISON APPLE
PRESS

Dear reader,

I'm so excited to have you here with me on all of my adventures. As you know, my adventures with magical stories ended in the Cave of Stories, but your adventures can continue on!

This writing journal has everything you need to create your own litearary adventures.

Happy writing and remember to always believe in fairytales!

LOVE, ELEANOR

1

If you could travel to any magical place, where would you go?

_____

_____

_____

_____

_____

_____

_____

_____

"Imagination is the only weapon in the war with reality."

- Lewis Carroll, 'Alice in Wonderland'.

2

Who is your main character(s)?
Describe them below

_____

_____

_____

_____

_____

_____

_____

_____

_____

Sketch it out!

"They can't order me to stop dreaming."

-'Cinderella'.

3

It's time to create the villain!

_____

_____

_____

_____

_____

_____

_____

_____

_____

_____

Sketch it out!

"I want adventure in the great wide somewhere!
I want it more than I can tell!"
'Beauty And the Beast'.

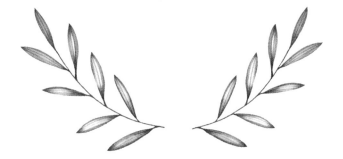

If your main character could have any sidekick what/who would they have? Describe them below

_____

_____

_____

_____

_____

_____

_____

_____

5

The last thing we have to think about is if the characters have any super powers/magic in this place you've created.

_____

_____

_____

_____

_____

_____

_____

_____

_____

Sketch it out!

you're doing great!

Okay, this is where I leave you to create! Now that you've gotten all of the basics, it's time to start writing.

LOVE, ELEANOR

Once upon a time...

Made in the USA
Monee, IL
16 February 2022

91351268R00039